American edition published in 2021 by Andersen Press USA,
an imprint of Andersen Press Ltd.
www.andersenpressusa.com

First published in Great Britain in 2021 by Andersen Press Ltd.,
20 Vauxhall Bridge Road, London SW1V 2SA

Distributed in the United States and Canada by
Lerner Publishing Group, Inc.
241 First Avenue North
Minneapolis, MN 55401 USA

For reading levels and more information, look up this title at www.lernerbooks.com.

Library of Congress Cataloging-in-Publication Data Available
978-1-7284-4970-8 (LB)
978-1-7284-5636-2 (EB)

1–TL–9/1/2021

ELMER
and the Bedtime Story

David McKee

Andersen Press USA

Elmer the patchwork elephant was about to start an afternoon walk when two young elephants appeared, followed by their mother.

"Hello, Elmer," said the mother. "Please will you look after Stella and Mel? I have to visit my sister."

“I’ll be back late,” she continued. “You’ll have to put them to sleep. A story will do it, like the one about the flying carpet.” She left. “A tiring walk will do it as well,” chuckled Elmer. “Like the one we’re going on.”

They'd been walking for a while when a voice called, "Hello, Elmer! Are you babysitting as well?" It was Lion.
"Hello, Lion," said Elmer. "Yes I'm getting them tired so they'll sleep easily."

"Tell them a story, that will do it," said Lion.

"The one about the magic cookie," said the young lions.

Elmer smiled. "Magic cookie," he said. "I could make one vanish!"

The walk took them to the river.
"Are you babysitting as well, Elmer?"
called Crocodile.
"Hello, Crocodile," said Elmer. "Yes, I'm
getting them tired so that they'll sleep easily."

“Tell them a story,” said Crocodile. “That will do it.”
“Tell them about the monster who lost his shadow,”
said a young crocodile.

"Oh, poor monster," said Elmer and walked on.

"This is nice and tiring," thought Elmer as they climbed a hill. Stella and Mel raced ahead and back again.

"Babysitting, Elmer?" called Monkey.

"Yes, I'm getting them tired so they'll sleep easily," said Elmer

"Tell them a story, that will do it," said Monkey.
"The one about the echo," said a little monkey.
"ECHO, echo, echo, echo . . . " said Elmer with a smile.

Next it was Rabbit.
"Babysitting, Elmer?" he asked.
"Yes," said Elmer, "I've been getting them tired so they'll sleep easily."

"Tell them a story," said Rabbit. "That will do it."

"The one about the invisible teddy bear!" called a young rabbit.

"We'll see," said Elmer. "They must be tired because I am. We're nearly home."

Later at home, Elmer said, “It’s time to sleep.”
The youngsters settled down and said, “Please,
Elmer, tell us a story.”
Elmer yawned. Slowly he started, “Once upon a
time . . . there were two brave elephants . . .
called Stella and Mel . . .
one day . . .”

Elmer woke as the youngsters' mother arrived.
She smiled. "A good story always works," she said.

"So does a good walk," said Elmer. "I never got to 'And they lived happily ever after'!"